SILLY JOKES FOR 5 YEAR OLDS

CW00841122

What kind of bread do elves use for sandwiches?

A. Shortbread!

Which button can you not do up or undo?

Your belly button!

Do you know that squids can squirt rainbow ink?!

A. Only Squidding!

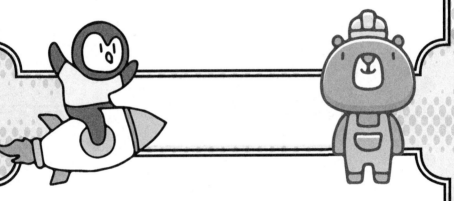

Which type of lion can't roar?

A dande-lion!

What is a flying turtle called?

A shell-icopter!

How do bumblebee's blow bubbles with candy?

With bumble gum!

What does a lion say when it meets other animals in the wild?

I'm very pleased to eat you!

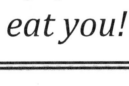

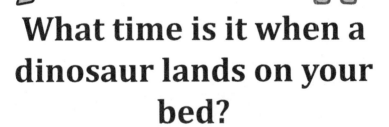

What time is it when a dinosaur lands on your bed?

It's time you get out of your bedroom!

Knock, knock.
Who's there?
A leaf.
A leaf who?
A leaf you in peace if you leaf me in peace!

What should you do if a dinosaur sneezes?

Get yourself out the way!

What does a princess do every single morning?

She wakes up, of course!

Why do you have to go to bed each night?

Because your bed can't come to you!

Knock, knock.
Who's there?
Double.
Double who?
W is my favorite letter!

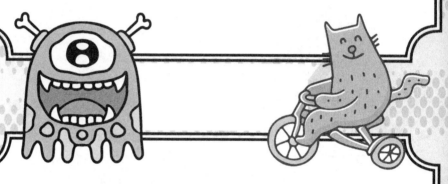

Why is a banana different from an elephant?

Because elephants aren't yellow, silly!

What pizza topping tastes like popcorn?

Pop-peroni!

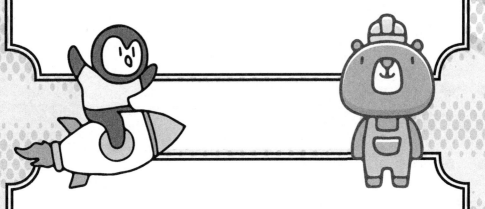

What is the Avengers' favorite day of the week?

THOR-sday!

Why wouldn't the dinosaur cross the road?

Because there weren't any roads!

What does a turtle wear when it goes mountain biking?

A shell-met!

What do you call a deer standing in heavy rain?

A rain-deer!

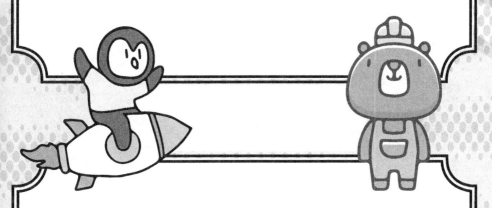

What would Thor say if Spider Man was annoying him?

Don't bug me, man!

What would a nose say to a finger?

Stop picking on me!

What happened when the monster took the school bus all the way home?

He had to carry it back!

Why do birthday candles go on top of the cake?

Because they can't go on the bottom!

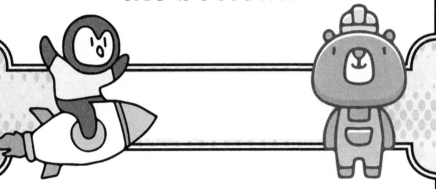

What's the best thing you can put into a cake?

Your teeth!

What footwear is best for ghosts?

BOO-ts!

What is red and has to sit in the corner?

A fire engine when it's been naughty!

What does a cow read to find the latest news?

A mooooo-spaper!

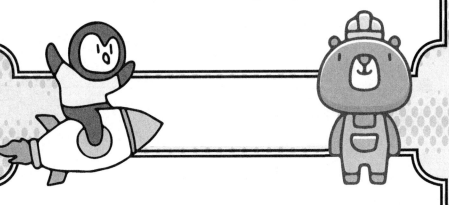

What is wobbly, small and cries everyday?

A jelly baby!

Knock, knock.
Who's there?
Zero want.
Zero want who?
3, 4!

What game does a mouse love to play?

Hide and Go Squeak!

What is a smurf's favorite type of cheese?

Blue cheese!

How can a rabbit fly?

By taking a hare-plane!

What would you call a dog that loves playing in the rain?

A soggy doggy!

Which snack always gives you a loud surprise?

POP-corn!

What happens when you cross a kangaroo with a Triceratops?

You get a Tricera-hops!

What did the mouse whisper to the cat?

Nothing. It just ran away!

What sort of cake can you get from the trash?

A bad stomach-cake!

What can you call a rabbit that tells lots of jokes?

Funny bunny!

What is a velociraptor's favorite thing in a playground?

The dino-see-saur!

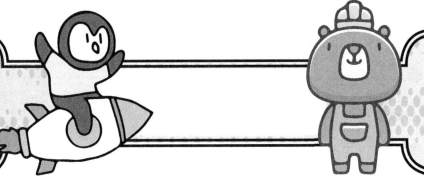

Which part of school do snowmen love best?

Snow and tell!

What would you find inside a ghost's nose?

Boo-gers!

Where would a diplodocus buy its groceries?

At the dino-store!

Why should you be careful if it's raining cats and dogs?

You don't want to step in a poodle!

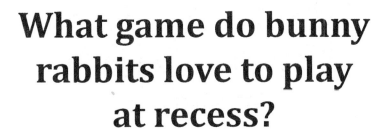

What game do bunny rabbits love to play at recess?

Hopscotch!

What is a cow's favorite Disney movie?

Moo-lan!

What cereal does a snowman have for breakfast?

Snowflakes!

What does a bee say to their friend?

I like bee-ing friends with you!

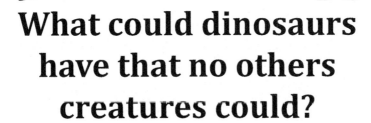

What could dinosaurs have that no others creatures could?

Dinosaur babies!

What is a cow's favorite kind of rock?

A mooooo-n rock!

Knock, knock.
Who's there?
I'm Justin.
I'm Justin who?
I'm Justin time to try those cookies you baked!

What sort of room has no door?

A mushroom!

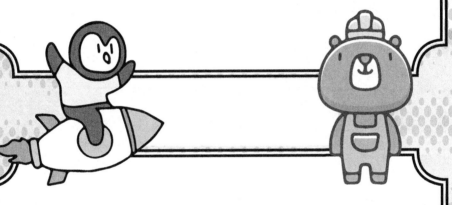

What type of shoes do grizzly bears wear?

None; they always go bear foot!

Knock, knock.

Who's there?

Orange.

Orange who?

**Orange you happy
I came to see you?!**

**How could you tell if an
elephant is living in your
cupboard?**

*You won't be able to
shut the door!*

Where does an octopus go when it is sick?

To see the doctor-pus!

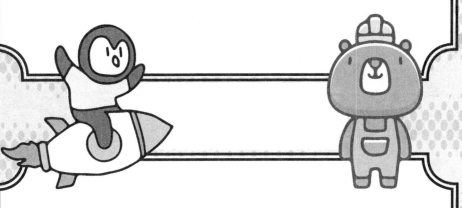

What's black and white and goes up and down all day?

A penguin stuck in an elevator!

Knock, knock!
Who's there?
H-h-hatch.
H-h-atch who?
Oh dear, bless you!

Where was the zebra after the sunset?

It was in the dark!

What kind of candy do frog's love to lick?

A lolli-hop!

If a burp had a color, what would it be?

Burple!

Where do they teach you how to make ice cream?

At sundae school!

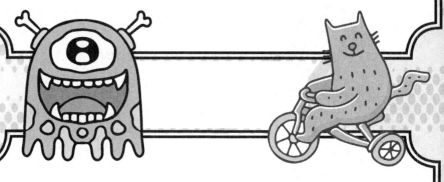

What has three horns and three wheels?

A triceratops on a tricycle!

What did the octopus say to her octopus friend?

Do you want to hold my hand, hand, hand, hand... hand, hand, hand, hand?

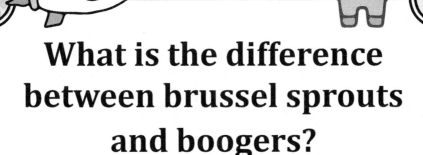

What is the difference between brussel sprouts and boogers?

Kids never eat brussel sprouts!

What kind of chocolate do cows eat?

Moo-teasers!

Why couldn't the monkey stop eating bananas?

Because it's a monkey!

What does a frog feel when it loses its legs?

Quite unhoppy!

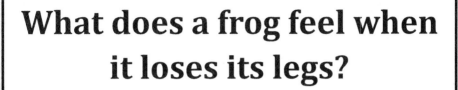

Which card game is a crocodile's favorite?

Snap!

Knock, knock.
Who's there?
Didgeridoo.
Didgeridoo who?
**Did you read two of the
Peppa Pig books or three?!**

**Where should you look for
fruit at a fair?**

The cherry-go-round!

What is the best name for a snowman in summer?

Puddle!

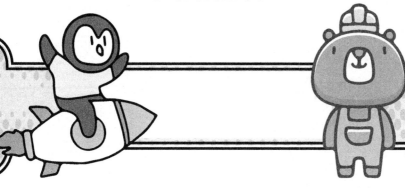

Which is a the most popular Christmas carol for monkeys?

Jungle Bells!

What makes cows great at math?

They are excellent at cow-nting!

What made the chicken cross the road?

It needed to get to the other side!

Which furry pet smiles the most?

Grinny-pigs!

Knock, knock.
Who's there?
Isabella.
Isabella who?
Isabella not working?
I've been ringing like crazy!

What made the monkey fall off her bicycle?

She slipped off her banana seat!

What should you call a sheep that can dance?

A baaaa-lerina!

Which US city has the most cows?

Moo York City!

What happened to the ghost after it fell?

It got a painful boo-boo!

Did you hear about that very silly sailor?

He put on a gravy uniform instead of a navy uniform!

Which two party games do cows love to play?

Moo-sical chairs and moo-sical statues!

What kind of monkey has eight legs?

A spider monkey!

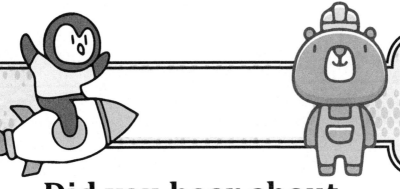

Did you hear about that other sailor who loved vegetables?

They sailed the high peas instead of the high seas!

What do owls say when they're out doing trick or treat?

Happy Owl-oween!

Where is a monkey's favorite place to exercise?

A jungle gym!

What does a traffic warden love in their sandwiches?

Lots of traffic jam!

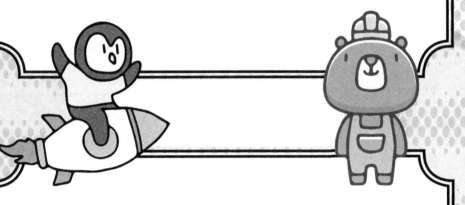

What would a cow driver say if you go near their car?

Mooooo-ve over!

What school subject do pirates love?

Arrrrr-t!

Which type of fruit can fix a broken toilet?

A plum-ber!

On which night do more werewolves appear?

Halloween!

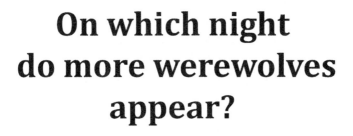

What kind of monkey can fly?

A hot air baboon!

What do cows love to pour on their pancakes?

Moo-ple Syrup!

What kind of vehicle does the boogeyman drive?

A monster truck!

Who delivers Christmas presents to the beach?

Sandy Claws!

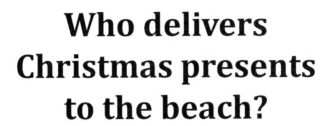

What does a librarian use to catch fish?

Book worms!

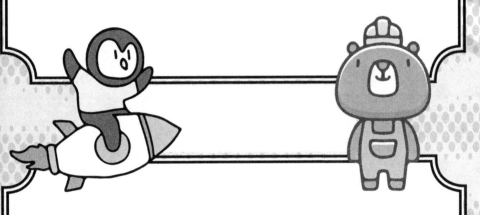

If a monkey is holding 15 bananas in his left hand and 15 bananas in his right, what does he have?

Really huge hands!

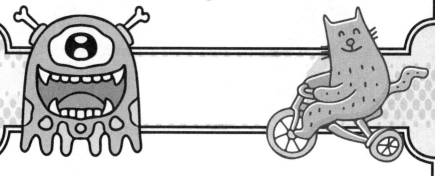

Which type of candy are teachers' favorites?

Smarties!

Why did the dog want to stay in the shade?

She didn't want to become a hot dog!

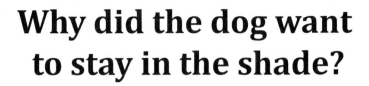

Which building has more stories than any other?

The library!

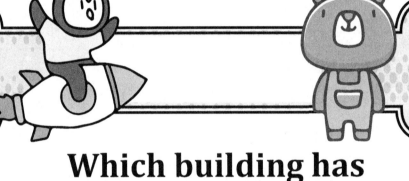

What was Zuma from Paw Patrol's Halloween costume?

A hot dog!

Why did the sheep have to cross the road?

Because the chicken wanted a day off.

How does a firefighter catch a stray monkey?

They climb up a tree and go bananas!

Which letter of the alphabet is hot when you drink it?

T!

Which fruit do ghosts love best?

Boo-berries

What would you call a monkey in the North Pole at Christmas?

A cold lost monkey!

Which type of ball can't bounce?

A snowball!

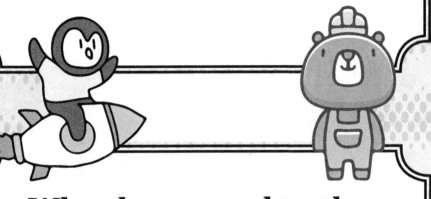

What happened to the lioness after she ate a clown?

Her belly felt funny!

How do trains eat?

They go chew chew!

What do puppies use to move their boat?

Doggy paddles!

What makes a lot more noise than a rocketship?

Ten rocket ships!

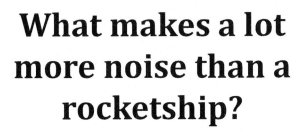

What do monkeys love to bake?

Banana bread!

Where is the best place to wait to see a lion on safari?

Inside your car!

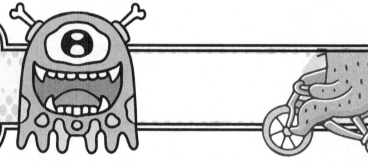

Why should you not eat your Halloween candy all at once?

Because you need to leave room for ice-scream!

What does Peppa Pig always do when she gets home from school?

Her ham-work!

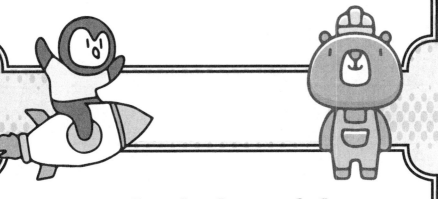

On which day of the week do tigers eat the most food?

Chews-day!

What is Daddy Pig's favorite sporting event to watch on TV?

The Olym-pig Games!

What do pigs love to do when it's sunny?

Have pig-nics!

When monkeys become ghosts, which fruit do they love to eat?

Boo-nanas!

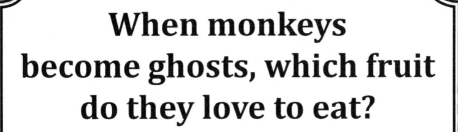

Knock, Knock.
Who's there?
Ice cream.
Ice cream who?
Ice cream louder than anyone else!

What happens when you cross Daddy Pig with a cactus?

You get Daddy Pork-upine!

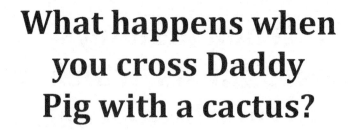

How can someone bring the Moon down to Earth?

In their dreams!

Knock, Knock.
Who's there?
Ben.
Ben who?
Benanas are the best!

Which dog is the best at telling the time?

A watch-dog!

Knock, Knock.
Who's there?
Felix.
Felix Who?
Felix-cited to go trick-or-treating on Halloween!

Why did the swan cross the road?

Because she was the chicken's best friend!

Why can't Christmas trees stand up?

Have you ever seen a Christmas tree with legs?!

What is yellow and goes up, down, up, down?

A lemon in an elevator!

Which bird always wins a gold medal at the Winter Olympics?

A peng-win!

How can a group of penguins make a decision?

They can flipper coin!

What is green, but not very heavy?

Light green!

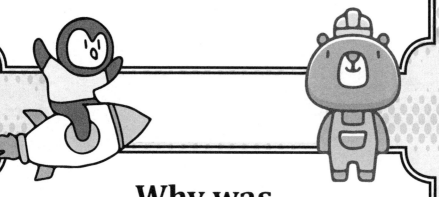

Why was the belt arrested?

It was holding up some pants!

What brings lots of cows to New York?

They love going to watch moo-sicals!

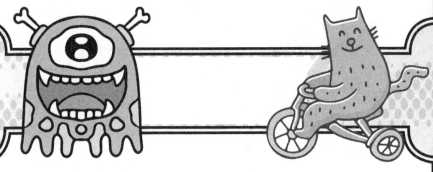

Why are scissors so good at running races?

Because they know all the shortcuts!

What happens to Batman when he tells a joke?

He turns into
The Joker!

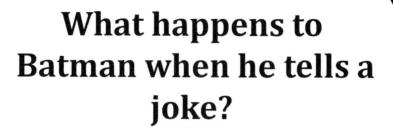

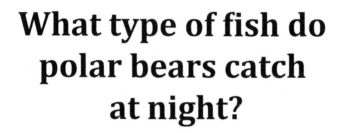

What type of fish do polar bears catch at night?

Star-fish!

What would you call a duck that always robs things?

A robber ducky!

When is a penguin happiest?

When they give you a pen-grin!

Why are cows so good at adding?

Because they always use their cow-culators!

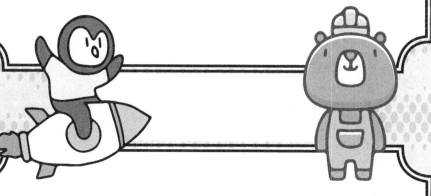

What is a Tyrannosaurus-Rex allowed to eat?

Anything that it wants to!

How can you get Santa Claus to stop moving?

Press Santa Pause!

How can you tell if a cow is a great dancer?

You have to see if the cow has any good mooo-ves!

Where do ducks go when they feel sick?

To visit the duck-tor!

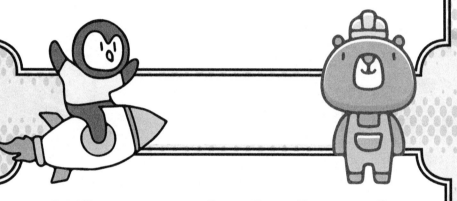

Why was the little girl so chilly on Christmas eve?

Because it was the middle of Decem-brrr!

How does a goldfish smell?

It smells pretty fishy!

What will you get when you fill a box with ducks?

You get a box full of quackers!

Why is everyone friends with Frosty the Snowman?

Because he's a very cool guy!

Which vegetable has the smelliest feet?

Pota-toes!

Printed in Great Britain
by Amazon

51822279R00046